W9-BGR-343

Ex Libris, Friends of
Lake County Public Library

ABOUT THE BANK STREET READY-TO-READ SERIES

More than seventy-five years of educational research, innovative teaching, and quality publishing have earned The Bank Street College of Education its reputation as America's most trusted name in early childhood education.

Because no two children are exactly alike in their development, the Bank Street Ready-to-Read series is written on three levels to accommodate the individual stages of reading readiness of children ages three through eight.

● *Level 1:* GETTING READY TO READ (Pre-K–Grade 1)
Level 1 books are perfect for reading aloud with children who are getting ready to read or just starting to read words or phrases. These books feature large type, repetition, and simple sentences.

● *Level 2:* READING TOGETHER (Grades 1–3)
These books have slightly smaller type and longer sentences. They are ideal for children beginning to read by themselves who may need help.

○ *Level 3:* I CAN READ IT MYSELF (Grades 2–3)
These stories are just right for children who can read independently. They offer more complex and challenging stories and sentences.

All three levels of the Bank Street Ready-to-Read books make it easy to select the books most appropriate for your child's development and enable him or her to grow with the series step by step. The levels purposely overlap to reinforce skills and further encourage reading.

We feel that making reading fun is the single most important thing anyone can do to help children become good readers. We hope you will become part of Bank Street's long tradition of learning through sharing.

The Bank Street College of Education

3 3113 01670 5909

For my Annie,
with love
—E.S.

To my sister Dianne
—J.C.

SWIM LIKE A FISH

A Bantam Book/June 1997

Published by Bantam Doubleday Dell Books
for Young Readers, a division of Bantam
Doubleday Dell Publishing Group, Inc.
1540 Broadway, New York, New York 10036.

Special thanks to Evelyn Johnson and Kathy Huck.

The trademarks "Bantam Books" and the
portrayal of a rooster are registered
in the U.S. Patent and Trademark Office
and in other countries. Marca Registrada.

All rights reserved.
Copyright © 1997 by Byron Preiss Visual Publications, Inc.
Text copyright © 1997 by Bank Street College of Education.
Illustrations copyright © 1997 by John Cymerman
and Byron Preiss Visual Publications, Inc.

No part of this book may be reproduced or transmitted
in any form or by any means, electronic or mechanical,
including photocopying, recording, or by any information
storage and retrieval system, without permission in writing from
the publisher.
For information address: Bantam Books

ISBN: 0-553-37583-0

Published simultaneously in the United States and Canada
PRINTED IN THE UNITED STATES OF AMERICA
0 9 8 7 6 5 4 3 2 1

Swim Like a Fish

by Ellen Schecter
Illustrated by John Emil Cymerman

A Byron Preiss Book

LAKE COUNTY PUBLIC LIBRARY

BANTAM BOOKS
NEW YORK · TORONTO · LONDON · SYDNEY · AUCKLAND

It was HOT!
It was so hot you could
fry eggs on the sidewalk.

Annie sat on her stoop.
She felt like she might melt.
Mama came out, fanning herself
with the morning paper.
"Let's go swimming," she said.

"But I can't swim," said Annie.
"You couldn't last year.
But you can learn.
I'll help you," said Mama.
"You'll be swimming like a fish
before you can say 'Hot diggity.'"

So Mama and Annie
jumped into their suits.
They packed up a picnic
and headed for the pool.

Annie dipped her big toe in
the cool blue water.
Then she pulled it out again.
She was scared.

Mama jumped in with both feet.
She splashed cool silver drops
up at Annie.
"Come on in!" said Mama.

10

"It's nice and cool.
Don't worry—it's not deep.
And I'll hold you the whole time."
But Annie was still scared.

Mama smiled
and held out her hands.
Annie climbed down the ladder
inch by inch by inch.

She grabbed Mama's hands
and held on tight.
Mama helped Annie float.
"Let's pretend we're fish.
Watch me!" said Mama.

Mama floated just like a fish.
So did Annie.
Then they made funny fish faces.
They fluttered their fins.

They blew bubbles
and chased them
down to the bottom
and up to the top.

"I can do it!" said Annie.
"I can float and flutter
and bubble and blow —
just like a fish!"

"What's next?" asked Annie.
"Can you paddle like a puppy?"
asked Mama.
"I think so," said Annie.

Annie let go of Mama's hands.
Then she paddled with her paws.
She sniffed with her nose.
She even wagged her tail.

So did Mama.
They paddled like puppies
all the way across the pool.
"I did it!" barked Annie.

"You did it!" clapped Mama.
"Is it my turn to choose?"
asked Annie.

"It's your turn!" smiled Mama.
"Then let's dive like dolphins!"
said Annie.

"Let's slide through the sea
in our silvery skins.
Let's leap in the waves
and play all day.

Let's squeak and call
in our own secret code."
And that's just what they did!

"Now let's sneak like sharks!"
whispered Annie.
"Let's snap our jaws
and our sharp white teeth.

Let's sneak through the sea and scare all the fish!"

So, silent as shadows,
they swam side by side
in search of their snack.

27

Now Annie let go of Mama.
She paddled with her hands
and kicked with her feet.
She swam in a circle
all the way around Mama.

28

They laughed and hugged.
Then Annie splashed
rainbow drops
all over Mama.

"Look at me, Mama!"
said Annie.
"I can float
like a fish!

I can paddle like a puppy!

I can dive like a dolphin!

I can sneak like a shark!"

"Hurray for you!" hollered Mama.
"Hot diggity dog!" Annie cheered.
"Now I can swim all by myself
like a big, brave, grown-up girl!"

32

JUV E SCHE   CL
Schecter, Ellen.
Swim like a fish

LAKE COUNTY PUBLIC LIBRARY
INDIANA

AD	FF	MU
AV	GR	NC
BO	HI	SJ
CL JAN 0 6 '98	HO	CN L
DS	LS	

THIS BOOK IS RENEWABLE BY PHONE OR IN PERSON IF THERE IS NO RESERVE
WAITING OR FINE DUE.

LCP #0390